P9-CBQ-886

THE HAMMERHEADS OF TREASURE ISLAND

by Geoffrey T. Williams

Photography/Tom Campbell

Illustrated by
Artful Doodlers

save our seas
FOUNDATION

For more information about the Save Our Seas Foundation,
please visit our website at
www.SaveOurSeas.com

Book designed and packaged by Jokar Productions, LLC

No part of this publication may be reproduced in whole or in part,
or stored in a retrieval system, or transmitted in any form or by any means,
electronic, mechanical, photocopying, recording, or otherwise,
without written permission of the publisher.

For information regarding permission, write to Save Our Seas Foundation,
Attention: Permissions Department, 6 rue Bellot, 1206 Geneva, Switzerland

ISBN 978-0-9800444-2-3

©2010 Save Our Seas Foundation

All rights reserved. Published by SAVE OUR SEAS LIMITED.
Team SOS, Save Our Seas Foundation, and colophon
are trademarks and/or registered trademarks of SOS Ltd.

10 9 8 7 6 5 4 3 2 1

Printed China

ONE

KILLERS

The powerful cutter knifed through the water, passing Cocos Island and Chatham Bay to the south. Foam sprayed high and wide as it slammed through the waves. Xochitl Meléndez stood on the bow, watching through high-powered binoculars, as the fishing boat in the distance grew closer.

The captain, standing next to the girl had to yell over the roar of the engines. "Es que el barco?"

Xochitl—called Show by her friends—nodded, her long, black hair blowing back in the wind. "Sí. The Foundation's been tracking the boat for over a week now. We figure they've taken more than a hundred hammerheads so far."

The Save Our Seas Foundation had provided the long-range patrol boat to Costa Rica's conservation department—the Sistema Nacional de Areas de Conservación (SINAC)—and to the Costa Rican Navy, to help stop illegal fishing around Cocos Island. The tiny island, about 500 kilometers west of Costa Rica in the Eastern Pacific, is one of that country's national parks, and a world-famous underwater paradise. It is home to thousands of tiburones martillo—hammerhead sharks. They are protected by Costa Rica and most other countries around the world. In all the world's oceans, sharks are becoming an endangered species. By some estimates, the hammerhead shark population has decreased by over ninety percent in just the past thirty years.

Show, the Foundation's agent in Mexico and Central America, had a special place in her heart for the hammerheads of Cocos Island. Her family had been coming here to dive since she was a little girl. Watching the underwater parade of hundreds of these exotically-shaped sharks passing by overhead was one of the most beautiful, strange, and wondrous sights she had ever seen. She never tired of it.

They were almost on top of the fishing boat, which had made no attempt at escape, knowing they could never outrun the faster cutter. Minutes later, SINAC inspectors were aboard examining the hold of the fishing boat.

It was even worse than Show had feared. The inspectors found twenty seven hammerheads, twelve whitetip reef sharks, and six giant mantas. The greed and cruelty of the poachers made her want to cry. Because shark meat is almost worthless, the animals are killed for their fins, which are dried and sold at high prices in Asian markets for the quasi-medicinal market and use in shark-fin soup.

They arrested the crew and took the boat in tow.

On the way back to Costa Rica, the cutter dropped Show off at her sailboat, the *Poco Gitana*, anchored in Bahia Yglesias, on the south side of Cocos. She and some friends would be able to spend a few days diving. She hoped the timeless wonder of Cocos Island's sea life would ease the ache in her heart.

TWO

FEEDING FRENZY

Show waited patiently, lazy bubbles from her scuba tank weaving toward the surface where bright sunlight penetrated the blue waters of the bay. She motioned to her friends to wait just a little longer. Experience told her that conditions were right. She could see dolphins, silky sharks, big jacks, tuna, and thousands upon thousands of sardines—otherwise known as baitfish.

You can't have a bait ball without baitfish.

It started slowly. The dolphins, tuna, and jacks circled the widely spread-out school of baitfish. In a large group, safety lies at the center. The baitfish, sensing danger from the predators, began swimming toward each other, forming a loose sphere.

The predators circled around and around, herding the small fish together. The sphere grew larger and more tightly packed as more and more sardines huddled together. In minutes, thousands of frantic fish had become a swirling mass of desperation, each individual trying to escape to the center of the whirling ball. Streaming ribbons of sunlight turned the bait ball into a silvery, spinning, flashing mirror of light.

The feeding frenzy began. The jacks and tuna darted in. The dolphins joined them. The silky sharks attacked like torpedoes, flying into the ball, their hungry mouths open, heads twisting from side to side, jaws snapping open and closed.

The whirling ball stretched all the way to the surface, stirring up the water in that part of the bay. That's when the birds joined the party. Frigates, terns, noddys, and red-footed boobies swooped and dived, skimming meals off the churning surface.

It was an amazing sight. Show had seen bait balls in which the predators ate every single fish, down to the last one.

But not this time.

This time, something changed. Suddenly. Violently.

Show was surprised when the dolphins leaped away. An instant later, the sharks, jacks, and tuna scattered. The bait ball broke up, disintegrating, into small groups of tiny fish.

Show had never seen anything like it before. What could cause this? she wondered.

Then the sound reached her. A series of low, almost subsonic booms. Moments later her body was shaken. It felt like being in the grip of a giant fist. Waves of underwater percussion beat against her. She could see her friends, their bodies being thrown about almost uncontrollably in the surging water. Earthquake! the girl thought. An underwater earthquake!

After a few, frightening moments, it ended. She didn't want to wait for aftershocks. She signaled her friends, and they made for the surface and the safety of the boats.

THREE

El Dorado Sueño

This is an A.I. Notice. You have incoming live video."

Alena Worthy switched the call to the big high-definition monitor in the *Sea Worthy*'s lounge. A moment later she was looking at the smiling face of one of her best friends.

She called Tyler into the lounge. "Hey! We have a call from Show."

Her twin brother came running into the room. "Hey, Show!"

The girl smiled. Her face was still wet from diving, and she was drying her long hair with a beach towel. "Hey Tyler. Alena. You guys can't believe the hammerhead schools around Cocos this year. Dozens of those beautiful, strange creatures. And we saw a bait ball the size of a hot air balloon, so close to the surface, even the birds joined in."

"Your friends still there with you?" Tyler said.

"They sailed back yesterday. We had some great dives. Sure wish you could have made it."

"We had some business to take care of in Florida," explained Alena. "Just got back a few days ago."

"You'll probably hear about it from the Foundation," began Show, "but we helped SINAC and the Costa Rican Navy put another illegal fishing boat out of operation."

Alena clenched her jaw. "How bad was it?"

"Almost a hundred hammerheads, some whitetips, and giant mantas."

"Good thing you stopped them," Tyler said. "You heading back to Baja?"

"Yeah." Her bright smile faded. "But there's something else here I need to check out first."

"No solo diving, right?" Alena said to her friend.

"No way. There was an underwater earthquake yesterday—at least I thought it was an earthquake. But when I checked the National Oceanic and Atmospheric Administration (NOAA) web site, there was no report. I saw this big yacht, El Dorado Sueño."

"The golden dream," Alena said.

Show nodded. "Yeah. They're probably just amateur treasure hunters."

"Always been a lot of them on that little island," Tyler said.

"Lots of treasure, too," said Alena.

Show nodded. "Anyway, I tried to raise them on the radio. See if they'd felt anything. Got no response. So I took the dingy alongside and…" She shrugged.

Now Tyler was curious. "And what? What's the deal?"

"And nothing. I yelled. No one answered. Tried the radio again. Still nothing. Like it was deserted. I want to check it out some more. If I find out anything, I'll call."

"Call no matter what you find out," Alena said.

They disconnected a few minutes later with the kind of promises good friends who are separated make to each other—to get together soon, laugh more, talk more.

But it didn't quite work out that way…

FOUR

RED ALERT

It was a great day for sailing. Alena and her friend Addison Regan were running close on the wind, spray from the plunging bow slicing through the white caps just outside the Santa Barbara harbor. The mainsail and the jib were filled, and the small boat was trailing a long wake. With such beautiful weather and such fun company, it was easy to forget about Show's call.

"Get ready to come about," Addison said.

"Do I loosen the ropes now?" Alena was used to the *Sea Worthy*, a big, high-tech hydroplane, and was finding it hard remembering everything there was to remember about crewing on a small sailboat.

Addison laughed. "I keep telling you—they're not called ropes. On a sailboat they're called sheets. And no, don't release the sheet yet." He held the tiller, ready to pull it. "You set?"

Alena nodded.

Addison pulled the tiller. "Helm's alee!" The boat began a graceful arc through the water. "Now pull. And watch out for the boom."

"Boom?" Alena said. "What's a—"

"Duck!"

With the boat's change in direction, the wind pushed the boom—the heavy shaft that the mainsail was attached to—across the boat, nearly whacking Alena in the head. She ducked just in time.

"Boom," Addison said with a small grin.

Things settled down after that. The breeze eased off. Alena relaxed, enjoying the salt air, the sun, and Addison's company. The twins had known him since they were all in the third grade. Next year they'd be juniors in high school. Alena and Addison had just started hanging out a few months ago. They shared a lot of interests, including scuba diving. Addison had been aboard the *Sea Worthy* several times when the Aquatic Intervention (A.I.) team went out to perform its regular inspection of the Channel Island's fragile environment. He knew a little about their work, and was curious to know more.

"You and Tyler do more than check out the islands, right? I mean, you were gone most of the summer."

"The Foundation sends us all over the place. We spent most of the summer in Dubai and Florida," explained Alena.

"Wow. That's some serious traveling. Just checking stuff out?"

For an instant, her mind flashed back a few weeks earlier to Florida's Ten Thousand Islands. The team had been trying to save manatees from a huge, enraged poacher with the weird name of Billy Boat. She and Tyler had narrowly missed being run down by a pack of personal watercraft driven by his crew. But that's another story...

"It's sometimes a little more than just checking stuff out," Alena said.

As if to make her point, a piercing tone split the quiet, followed by a thin, computerized voice.

"This is an A.I. Red Alert. This is not a drill. Repeat. This is an A.I. Red Alert."

"What's that?!" said Addison, staring in surprise at what he had thought was just a fancy watch Alena was wearing.

Instead of answering, she pushed a button on the side of the high-tech communication device, which her brother had designed and built. The computerized voice was replaced by Tyler's, sounding almost in a panic.

"You've gotta get back here. Like right now. I'm running through the flight check. We're almost ready to leave."

"Why? What's happening?" Alena said.

"It's Show. No time to explain now. Just get back here."

FIVE

A.I. ON THE WAY

Alena is the leader of the Foundation's A.I. team. Tyler is pilot, engineer, and, according to Alena, "Chief Science Geek." The Foundation sends them, and Brutus, their very clever Jack Russell terrier, all over the world to help protect the seas and the amazing animals that live in it. The Foundation is headquartered in Geneva, Switzerland. Their web site (http://www.saveourseas.com) is packed with pictures, movies, and fascinating information.

Tyler was waiting anxiously as Alena climbed aboard the *Sea Worthy*, followed by Addison. "Sorry, Addy," began Tyler. "We're leaving in just a few minutes and we don't have time to—"

"He's coming with us," Alena said. "I checked with headquarters."

"But this could get dangerous," said Tyler. "And he doesn't know anything about our work."

"I'll learn," replied Addison. "Besides, from what Alena's told me, you might need an extra pair of hands."

Tyler nodded, all business now. "Okay, then. Follow me. Sis, you check the lab and our supplies. But hurry." Addison followed him forward to the flight deck.

Alena went below and quickly checked that the *Nous Venons* was tied down. They rarely went anywhere without the small, fast submarine. Arky and The Claw, their very special remotely-operated vehicles, were secure against a bulkhead in the lab. The supercomputer was powered down. All breakables were carefully stored. But the most important thing—the Walkers Stem Ginger Biscuits were…were…gone!

She couldn't believe it. They never went anywhere without their favorite snack. "Tyler," she muttered to herself.

There were none of Tyler's usual jokes about Flight Attendants and barf bags, she noticed. This must be serious.

Moments later, Alena settled into the co-pilot's seat next to Tyler. Brutus was already buckled into the navigator's seat, wearing his custom-designed helmet and headset.

Addison looked at Brutus with an amused smile on his face, but the team's Security Officer, wasn't going to be dissed by a newcomer, friend or not. His lips curled back and he bared his sharp teeth and snarled. The helmet pushed his eyes into narrow slits, and he looked almost ferocious.

Addison pulled away a little, muttering, "Sorry." He nervously settled into the seat next to the terrier, which politely accepted the apology and was now looking at him with his usual doggy grin, his tongue hanging out of his mouth like a quarter-pound of bacon.

"What's with the seatbelts?" Addison asked. "I know this is a fast boat, but do we really need them?"

Tyler turned and glanced at him, smiling. Then he pushed some buttons on the console. Hydraulics whooshed and servo motors whined. Outside, wings unfolded from recesses along the sides of the *Sea Worthy*, turning the hydroplane into a jet airplane. Tyler pushed more buttons and the cabin was filled with the hushed sounds of powerful engines warming up. "You buckled in?" he said, as he shoved the throttles forward. The engines roared, and they took off across the water, pinning a thoroughly astonished Addison back in his seat.

Moments later they were airborne.

"Hold on, Show," Alena said to herself. "*Nous venons.*"

It was the team's unofficial slogan. In French, it means we're coming.

SIX

UP TO SPEED

Minutes later they were cruising at an altitude of 8,000 meters and a speed of nearly 600 kilometers an hour.

"So. Tell me. What's going on?" asked Alena. "What's happened to Show? Who sent the Red Alert?"

"I did," Tyler said. "I wasn't here when her call came through. I didn't get it until I got back aboard. Watch." He punched a button on the console.

The recording started playing back. Show's worried face filled the screen. "I wish you guys were here. I know this sounds crazy, but I think someone's killing the hammerheads. And it's not just illegal fishing. I think that earthquake was an underwater explosion. I heard another one last night. Sounded like it might have come from around Shark Fin Point. I think that ship, that El Dorado Sueño, has something to do with it, and that's where they're anchored. I'm around the point on the far side of Bahia Yglesias. Anyway, this morning I took the dingy out and found a bunch of dead fish, including some big hammerheads, floating by an underwater cave. All the tourist boats were gone. I could sure use some help to—hold on." She stopped and looked over her shoulder to something out of range of the camera. Then she looked back. "Felt like someone stepped aboard. Hang on while I… hey! What are you?" Her voice rose in a scared shout.

Alena still couldn't see what was happening, but she could hear. There was a tremendous crashing…another shout from Show…then nothing. The video blinked out. The screen went black, and the speakers blared static into the flight deck.

Addison was looking around like he didn't quite know what he had gotten himself into. "What just happened? Is that girl okay?"

"We'll find out. Believe me, we will find out." Alena turned to Tyler. "Headquarters?"

"Alerted just before you boarded."

"Then I better contact Laylah."

Laylah Bint Ansari was the Foundation's Senior Security Officer. She answered the call immediately even though it was past two o'clock in the morning in Geneva. She looked very worried.

"All we have is her last known location: 5° 30' 38.10" N, 87° 30 44.97" W. But that's just her boat. She doesn't have a personal data chip like you." All three of the A.I. team members had tiny GPS chips implanted just under their skin that reported their locations to the Foundation from anywhere in the world. "After this I think we'll make all our agents get them," said Ansari.

"Is there anyone in the area to help?" Alena asked.

"You're it."

"Thought so," Alena said. "Well, it's almost 5,000 kilometers to Cocos, so we've got eight hours to come up with a plan. We'll keep you up to speed."

Ansari nodded. "We'll contact the authorities in Costa Rica. Let them know what's going on. They have a couple of National Park agents at Chatham Bay. But I don't know how much help they'll be. We'll let you know if anything changes on our end." Her face faded from the screen as Alena disconnected.

Addison was shaking his head. "Will someone please get me up to speed? I'd like to know what's going on."

Alena gave him a brief rundown of what the team knew. It didn't take long since they didn't know much. Just the name of the boat, which Show had given them on her first call. And that wasn't proof of anything.

Addison said, "Okay. I get it. I'll try not to get in the way, and I'll try not to ask too many questions. But there may be ways I can help you." He smiled. "We've got a long trip. And I haven't eaten anything since before we took the sailboat out this morning. Anyone else hungry?"

Tyler pointed. "Galley's back that way."

A short time later Addison appeared carrying a tray with a heaping plate of tuna salad sandwiches, veggie chips, and tall glasses of milk. "And I found a box of these," he said, conjuring up a box of Walkers Stem Ginger Biscuits like a magician pulling a rabbit out of a hat.

Alena grinned, suddenly glad he was along.

"I've got a plan," said Alena as they began to eat. "Start at Bahia Yglesias and locate Show's boat. She would never abandon her Poco Gitana."

Tyler looked at his sister. "But if she's not there, we check out the rest of the island, right? All of it. Every bay and every rock. And we'll find that El Dorado Sueño."

Addison looked back and forth between the twins. "And then what?"

Tyler's eyes were hard and cold. "Then we'll ask someone some questions." His voice was so low that Addison had to strain to hear. He decided he wouldn't want to be the one having to answer those questions.

SEVEN

SEARCHNG FOR THE POCO GITANA

Tiny Cocos Island is the tip of an ancient volcano. It is known around the world as one of the most exciting places to dive. Jacques Cousteau, the famous ocean adventurer, called it the most beautiful island in the world. The water abounds with whale sharks, whitetip reef sharks, rays of all kinds, including giant mantas, green sea turtles, huge moray eels, tiger snake eels, red-lipped batfish, yellow trumpetfish, and undersea gardens of sea urchins, anemones, and coral.

But it is the hammerhead sharks that draw the divers. Almost nowhere else in the world will you find such a concentration of hammerheads in one place. These incredible animals roam the warm waters around the island in huge schools of two, three, even four hundred.

Over the years, Cocos has been visited by scientists, divers, presidents, and pirates. Lots of pirates. Some people say the island was Robert Louis Stevenson's inspiration for his classic pirate adventure Treasure Island.

Over the centuries, pirates drew maps of Cocos that told where to find hordes of buried treasure. There are rocks on the island where they carved names, dates, and drawings of their ships, along with skull and crossbones, now blurred and eroded from years of tropical rainstorms and earthquakes.

Some estimates say all the gold and jewels buried around the island are worth hundreds of millions of dollars. No wonder modern-day adventurers dream and scheme about striking it rich on Cocos.

The *Sea Worthy* reached the island at four in the morning. They had all taken turns napping, but Tyler was up and at the controls well before the others. It was pitch black outside, not even a moon to help him navigate. For many other pilots, it might have been a difficult approach and landing. But he had installed a new navigation device, and was eager to put it to use. It was a holographic head's-up-display—HUD for short.

Tyler punched in the island's latitude and longitude and let the *Sea Worthy*'s GPS system and the Foundation satellites do the rest. Within moments a luminous, semi-transparent 3D view of Cocos and the surrounding waters appeared in the air in the middle of the flight deck, with the *Sea Worthy*'s exact position indicated by the image of a tiny airplane. Tyler made an adjustment and now the island was shown from the approaching plane's point of view.

Alena joined her brother on the flight deck, walking through the holographic display to get to the co-pilot's seat. Brutus followed her, bouncing up into his seat. Addison came last, rubbing the sleep from his eyes. Then he was taken aback at the site of an ocean and island floating in the air.

"I'm going to set us down as close to Show's last known position as I can," Tyler said. He turned off the autopilot. Then, carefully watching the HUD and the instrument panel, he soon had them skimming just above the waters of Bahia Yglesias. They touched down smoothly as the light in the east was growing brighter.

By the time the *Sea Worthy* had transformed back into a hydroplane, and they had dropped anchor, it was bright enough to see outside.

They all went up on deck, looking around, expecting to see Show's pretty sailboat, the Poco Gitana, anchored nearby.

It was nowhere to be seen.

EIGHT

NEW FRIENDS

Tyler was standing next to a tall, shiny cylinder secured against an outer bulkhead in the *Sea Worthy*'s laboratory. He pushed a button on its side and after a moment, the hemispherical Plexiglas top began to glow with a pale, green radiance.

"Hello, Arky," Tyler said.

After Addison's long flight in a boat that turned into a plane, and the vision of a floating island in the middle of the cabin, he had decided that nothing about the A.I. Team was going to surprise him again.

Then he heard the cylinder answer Tyler.

"Hello. Tyler Worthy."

"How are you today?"

"All systems. Are go," Arky said.

"This is our friend, Addison Regan."

The high-resolution camera behind the Plexiglas dome rotated to look at the newcomer. "Hello, friend. Addison Regan." Arky stored Addison's image, voice, and name in his huge database of information.

Addison swallowed. "Uh. Hello."

"We have a mission for you, Arky." Tyler said.

"Mission. Good."

Arky, short for Autonomous Aerial Reconnaissance Craft, had been designed by Tyler, and built by Foundation engineers. He could fly for

hours at tremendous speed, look around for things the A.I. Team told him to search for, and send information back to the team's computers and communication systems. Arky was actually Arky-2. The first Arky had been shot down by pirates off the coast of South Africa. But that's another story...

"We need you to find Poco Gitana."

"Find Poco Gitana. Good." Arky answered. His memory banks included information for every Foundation agent around the world, so he knew everything about Show's sailboat, and could pick it out from among dozens of similar boats, even when he was flying at 310 kilometers an hour.

Tyler pointed and said, "Throw that switch over there, Addy."

Addison flipped the switch labeled Launch Control. A hatch slid open above Arky and a hydraulic platform lifted the drone up to the main deck.

Moments later they heard a hushed whoosh as Arky lifted off on his mission.

NINE

ABANDONED

The team was gathered around the communication console in the lounge, watching the video Arky was sending back, when something at the edge of the screen caught Addison's eye.

"Uh, Arky?" It felt a little strange talking to a machine.

"Yes. Friend Addison Regan."

And even stranger when the machine answered you by name. "I think I see something off to your left."

Arky turned to bring the image to center screen. "Yes. Friend Addison Regan. That is the Poco Gitana,"

"Good catch, Addy," Tyler said. "No wonder we didn't see it this morning. It's behind the Juan Bautista inlet."

They watched as the drone approached the large fist of rock sticking out of the bay less than half a kilometer on the southwest side of the island.

"Arky."

"Yes Alena Worthy."

"Slow down, circle, and send some close-ups."

"Slow down. Circle. Close-ups," Arky dutifully acknowledged.

The view of the sailboat grew larger. The boat was dead in the water, a depressing sight, with its sails hanging limply. The deck was tilted at a steep angle. Alena gasped. "It looks like she's sinking."

"There's no way Show's aboard," Tyler said. "She'd never leave it like that."

"Or she is aboard and can't do anything about it," Addison said, almost in a whisper.

None of them wanted to think about that.

Seconds later Tyler had fired up the *Sea Worthy*'s powerful engines, and the craft skimmed across the bay toward the stricken sailboat.

* * * * *

"What a beautiful boat," Addison said. "What does Poco Gitana mean?"

"Little gypsy," Alena said. "Show always admired Sir Francis Chichester."

"Sure! He sailed around the world alone in the Gipsy Moth. Set a bunch of records," said Addison.

"I think that's one of Show's dreams, too. I just hope she…" but she didn't finish the thought. Instead, she said, "Let's get over there."

Tyler helped them launch one of the small inflatables. He stayed aboard the *Sea Worthy* to monitor Arky.

As they approached the Poco Gitana, Alena was saddened by the look of the graceful sailboat. She was leaning awkwardly, grinding her starboard hull against the harsh rocks. There was a slack anchor line off the stern, but it had either pulled loose, or had been carelessly set in the first place. Show would never have allowed that, Alena thought.

Addison scrambled over the transom and gave Alena and Brutus a hand up. Brutus's claws scrabbled for traction on the sloping deck. It was quiet. Too quiet.

Alena was dreading what they might find. "What do you think, Brutus?" The terrier had a great instinct for danger. He looked up at her and, without hesitation, trotted down the steps to the interior.

The boat wallowed in the small waves, and Addison held Alena's arm to steady her as they followed the terrier. Brutus was waiting in the lounge at the bottom of the steps.

Inside, the Poco Gitana was comfortably and neatly furnished. Two staterooms, one at either end; two heads and a shower; a well-equipped galley that extended into the lounge they were standing in. Gleaming wood, shining chrome, clean, polished stainless steel.

And no sign of Show.

TEN

THE GOLDEN DREAM

"Arky."

"Yes. Tyler Worthy."

"I want to extend your mission."

"Extend mission. Good."

"Circumnavigate the island. We're looking for a ship—I don't know what kind, what color, anything. Probably a pretty good size cruiser—named El Dorado Sueño."

He watched the monitor as Arky turned past Shark Fin Point, continuing around Manta Corner. He passed Islas Dos Amigos, then Cabo Lionel, Punta Maria, and Cabo Barreto before finally coming to Wafer Bay.

Wafer Bay is famous in treasure-hunting lore. In 1820, the governor of Peru, fearing riots and a revolt against Spain by troops led by Simón Bolívar, entrusted British sea captain William Thompson with guarding the country's treasure. It consisted of two life-size statues of the Blessed Virgin and Divine Child cast in pure gold, 273 jeweled swords, tons of gold coins, and priceless jewelry—for a grand total of $60 million! The "Treasure of Lima," as it is now known, was far too tempting for Thompson to resist. He turned pirate, stole the vast treasure, loaded it onto his boat, the Mary Dear, and headed for Cocos where he supposedly buried it all.

Wafer Bay has a narrow beach, tall waterfalls tumbling off steep cliffs, and lush forest growing right up to the edge. The base of the cliffs are dotted here and there with dark tunnels, carved by the relentless pounding of the sea over thousands of years.

Near one of the dark openings, Tyler saw a long, gleaming shape on the water.

"Arky. Slow down a little. See that ship?"

"Yes. Tyler Worthy."

"Get me some close-ups."

The ship was immense—perhaps 50 meters—low and sleek, and, most unusual, jet black from the water line to the top of the superstructure. Even the windows had been blacked out.

No, not all black. Tyler realized, watching Arky's hi-resolution images. Gold paint trimmed the windows. And on the transom—black with gold lettering. El Dorado Sueño—The Golden Dream.

And it was definitely not deserted.

A door on the top structure opened, and two men appeared. One raised something, probably binoculars or a digital camera, to his eyes. The other raised …

"Arky! Get out of there. Now!"

"Getting out. Tyler Worthy. Now."

The ship's image dropped out of view as Arky went into a sudden climb and steeply-banked turn. Even so, Tyler clearly heard the blast of the gun as the man fired at the drone.

"Get home Arky. Now."

"Home. Yes. Tyler Worthy."

Tyler noted, with some interest, that it might just be possible for a machine to sound worried.

ELEVEN

RECONNAISSANCE AND REPAIRS

There's a sea valve in the hull," said Addison, climbing up from the hold. He had been checking out the Poco Gitana for signs of foul play. "Someone opened it. Tried to scuttle her. Didn't do a very good job."

"Is there much water?"

"I think if we can start the pumps we can get rid of what she's taken on."

Just then, Alena's wrist watch came to life.

"Alena. I need you over here." Tyler, sounding stressed.

"Be right there," she said. "Addy, can you take care of the pumps? Get this boat sailing again?"

He gave her a mock salute. "Aye, Skipper."

She smiled. "Brutus, you stay here and help. Okay?"

The terrier barked in agreement, and Alena hopped over the transom and into the inflatable, started the motor, and headed back to the *Sea Worthy*.

* * * * *

"A ship that size, you have to figure a crew of eight. Maybe more," said Tyler. He had briefed Alena on the situation with El Dorado Sueño.

"I have to believe Show's there," said Alena. "That is, if she's still—" She couldn't bring herself to think of any harm coming to their friend.

"She is on that ship," insisted Tyler. "They'd be crazy to hurt her,

wreck her boat, and then stick around like nothing happened." He looked at his sister. "You know what's next, right?"

She nodded. "Let's do it."

They hurried below to the *Nous Venons*. Alena started the pumps that flooded the special compartment, while Tyler climbed into the submarine and checked out all its systems.

Alena radioed Addison to let him know what was going on. He wasn't happy they were going without him. "It's just a look-see," she told him, wondering if she really believed it herself.

The compartment opened to the sea, the sub slid out, and the twins set out for Wafer Bay.

They ran in stealth mode, submerged the entire way. It cut down on their speed, but guaranteed their approach would be silent. It was almost ten kilometers eastward around the island from Bahia Yglesias to Wafer Bay.

Neither of them had ever been to Cocos before, and both wished they had come under other circumstances. The underwater life was spectacular. They passed beautiful corals, and clusters of garden eels weaved above the sandy bottom like thick grass. A monstrous whale shark swam by, its mouth, almost as wide as its body, gaping open to catch tiny plankton and fish. Several times, giant manta rays glided past in front of the sub, their enormous, yet graceful, wings carrying them through the water like ballet dancers.

As they passed Punta Maria, a school of scalloped hammerheads swam by, some up to almost four meters long. As they got closer, Tyler could see the four scallop-shaped lobes along the front edge of their heads that gave the species its name. "Easy to see why they're called hammerheads," he said.

Alena had done some reading about them. "Since their eyes and nostrils are so far apart, scientists think it increases their sensory abilities, and helps them find food and navigate."

"So how come they're always swinging their heads back and forth?" asked Tyler.

"Scientists think it helps them get more information about their surroundings," explained Alena.

"Wonder what they think about the shape of our heads."

Alena looked at her brother and smiled. "They call us roundheads."

TWELVE

SILENT RUNNING

Alena and Tyler were passing the entrance to Wafer Bay when the explosions hit them. The *Nous Venons* was picked up and shaken like a rug in a washing machine. Alena was knocked out of her seat and banged her head on the instrument panel. Tyler, piloting as usual, was still buckled in, and suffered nothing worse than a momentary jolt of fright. Sub-sonic booms echoed in the cabin of the small sub.

Tyler checked the instruments. "Definitely explosions. And close by."

"I'm fine, thanks for asking," said Alena, picking herself up off the deck and settling back into her seat, rubbing her head.

"Uh…sorry, sis," Tyler said, glad to see she was all right.

Minutes later, the *Nous Venons*'s instruments showed them the El Dorado Sueño still anchored where Tyler had last seen it. They stopped less than a hundred meters from the huge black ship, and floated just below the surface of the bay.

"Rig up the hydrophone," Tyler said. "Maybe I can pick something up, maybe even find out where they're keeping Show."

"You're going over there?"

"No other way to do it," he said, rigging up his rebreather system and getting ready to leave the sub.

In the gathering darkness, Tyler slid along the big ship just under the waterline, silent as smoke, and almost invisible in his black wetsuit,

full-face mask, and dark-colored rebreather system. He pressed the underwater microphone to the hull, listening carefully.

"—don't like it. What're we gonna do with her?"

"Nothing until the Captain says. You got those charges ready to go?"

"Yeah. But this blowing up stuff underwater. I don't think it's working too well."

"You're not paid to think. You're paid to blow stuff up. Don't think about the girl. Think about the gold."

"Yeah. I'll think about the gold."

Thank goodness, Tyler thought, Show's on the ship somewhere. But where? And why are they setting off explosions? He swam on, pausing when he heard other voices.

"—supposed to be in some hole. Or underwater cave."

"Yeah. But it's been two hundred years. Landslides, earthquakes… Island's a volcano, remember? Who knows? Something probably covered it up. The explosions are for seismic mapping. If there's a cave that's covered, the readouts will show it to us and—"

Earthquakes produce vibrations, called seismic waves, which travel through the ground. Scientists examine them to get information about the shape of the interior of the earth. Controlled explosions are used the same way: to find oil and gas deposits, old meteor craters, or buried treasure caves.

These people aren't amateurs, Tyler thought. That kind of technology would let them see behind and under the cliffs and rocks. It also means every underwater explosion they set off kills more animals. He moved on. So far, he had heard four men talking.

"—lobster not good enough for you?"

A different voice. A woman.

"I'm not hungry. When are you going to let me go?"

It's Show! She's okay! Tyler floated up to the surface as quietly as he could to mark his position relative to the ship. He was on the port side, about midship. There were several blacked-out windows above his head. He counted. The sixth window from the bow.

Now what? he thought. Gotta get more information. He moved along further and found himself under several large picture windows. Owner's stateroom, maybe. He pressed the hydrophone against the hull. Nothing. He was about to move on when he heard a thin voice, as though someone was talking over an intercom system.

"Sir. Sonar has picked up something off starboard. Too big to be a fish. Unless it's a whale shark. But it's not moving."

Then a deeper, older voice. With an accent, maybe Spanish. "Send someone down to check it out. I didn't like the look of that plane, or whatever it was, we saw today. I don't want anything or anyone interfering."

They've spotted the sub! I've got to get back! But she's on the other side, a hundred meters away! Don't panic. Gotta take a chance. Break radio silence.

He keyed the microphone built into his rebreather mask, and whispered. "Alena. They made you. You gotta get out of there now!"

"Not without you. I'm not leaving you behind!"

"You've got to. I found Show. I think I can get to her. They don't know about me yet. You've got to get back to the *Sea Worthy* and Addison. Then—" He stopped, hearing a rumbling sound from somewhere inside the big ship. Then a whining sound. He knew that sound. Electric motors. Like the type the *Nous Venons* used. El Dorado Sueño had a submarine!

"Go! Now!" he told his sister. "I'll be okay."

"But you've only got another hour's worth of air!"

"They've got a sub! GO!"

THIRTEEN

SHOW TIME

It started to rain.

That was fine with Tyler. In the darkness, the ship was a black wall looming above him. He swam toward the stern and found what he had expected: a ladder extending from the transom to the waterline. He climbed the ladder to the deck, then took off his awkward diving gear, stowing it carefully in the dark shadows under the ladder. He knew that one, maybe two men were still chasing Alena. He figured that left four or five men, and the woman on board along with Show. At least one man would be at the helm. Two were making explosives. Wouldn't it be nice to know where everyone was? Wouldn't it be nice if he could work things out so everyone would be in the same place at the same time...

The ship was over eight meters wide. A large inflatable boat hung from davits over part of the stern. Tyler made his way around a large dining table under an awning, next to a hot tub big enough for a baseball team. This was the biggest, fanciest yacht he had ever been on. It didn't seem right that it belonged to a criminal. He was about to open the door to the lounge when he had an idea.

He went back to the inflatable and quietly removed the tarp. The inflatable had a large center console, twin 200 horsepower engines, radar, depth finder, and autopilot. Perfect for what he had in mind. A power winch was used to raise and lower the boat. He jumped on board and started the winch, hoping it didn't make too much noise. It didn't.

Moments later, the boat was in the water, still attached to the cable. This next part would be noisy, he hoped. He turned the ignition key, hit the starter button, and the big outboard motor rumbled to life. Now! Quick! He turned on the autopilot and entered some random numbers. The engines were burbling in neutral. He put them in gear, unhooked the cable still holding the boat and jammed the throttles forward. The twin engines roared, the boat took off for the open ocean fast as a scalded cat, and just about as loud.

Tyler leaped over the side and scurried up the ladder, making it to the safety of the darkened walkway along the side of the lounge just as the lounge door banged open.

Four men hurried out, shouting at each other.

"Que pasa? What happened?"

"Who did that? Who took the boat?"

Then the man Tyler figured for the owner appeared. "Es la niña sigue en su cabina? The girl? She didn't escape?"

The woman appeared behind him. "La niña sigue ahí. She is locked in."

While they were all gathered at the stern, Tyler slipped through the door to the lounge. Wow! Talk about rich! Chandeliers hung from the ceiling, two curved staircases stood on either side of a giant bar and entertainment center, and polished wood was everywhere. He'd never seen anything like it. But this didn't seem the time to stop and admire it, so he hurried to the closest staircase. It went up to the next deck, and down into the ship. Tyler went down. A wide passageway ran along the center of the ship. He couldn't see any windows to count, so he had to guess. He opened a door. The room was empty. He tried the next door. Locked.

"Show?" he said in a loud whisper. "Show. It's Tyler."

"Tyler? Tyler, is that you?"

He smashed his shoulder against the door as hard as he could. Ow! That hurt! Not as easy as it looks on TV, Tyler thought. He slammed against it again and the door crashed open. Then Show was running toward him, tears streaming down her pretty face. She was so relieved she momentarily forgot her English.

"He intentado. He intentado tan duro," said Show.

"I know you tried to get away. Doesn't matter now. I'm just glad you're okay." He looked at her. She was barefoot, dressed in jeans and some kind of tank top. But she didn't look hurt. "You are okay, aren't you?"

"Bien. Estoy bien. I'm fine. Where's Alena?"

"No time now to explain. We have to get out of here."

She started down the hallway, the way he'd come.

"No. Not that way. They're all back there." He saw a narrow stairway ahead. "Can we get out that way?"

"They never let me out of that room. I don't know where that goes."

Shouts came from behind them. "Alto! Stop!" He looked back to see two men running after them.

"Well, we're about to find out." They sprinted down the passageway.

FOURTEEN

RUNNING SCARED

When Alena checked the sonar and saw the other submarine less than one hundred meters away, she forgot all about running silent. She revved up the motors, not worrying about stealth now.

She checked again. The other sub was closing in on her fast, less than twenty-five meters away. She jammed both throttles forward.

The race was on.

The *Nous Venons* was only slightly faster. But what if they follow me back to the *Sea Worthy*? she thought. I need an edge, something else. Or someone else.

She keyed her microphone. "Addison? Addy? If you're there, please answer." She held her breath. Maybe he hadn't been able to fix the *Poco Gitana*. Maybe he hadn't gotten back aboard the *Sea Worthy*. Maybe he didn't know how to operate the radio. Maybe -

"This is the *Sea Worthy*. I hope that's you, Alena."

She breathed a sigh of relief. "Thank goodness. I need a little help. Remember that ROV in the lab? The one Tyler called The Claw?"

Addison listened carefully to her instructions.

* * * * *

"Son demasiado rápido."

"Yes, they are fast. But we are almost as fast. They cannot lose us. Keep following. We will find where they are anchored."

"Sí. And then we will make Don Alejandro very pleased. They will learn no one must interfere with his treasure."

"¡Ai! ¿Qué es esa cosa?"

"No sé. I do not know what that is!"

Through the sub's small window they could see something moving toward them—something that looked like it could be from a movie about monsters from the deep. It had a rounded, slick body, bright, unblinking eyes, and, most frightening of all, long arms that ended in fierce-looking claws.

Alena docked the *Nous Venons* and rushed up to the lounge. Addison was sitting at the controls for The Claw. Its bright underwater lights had pinned the enemy sub like a bug under a microscope. "You better take over now," he said.

Normally, the A.I Team used The Claw for retrieving things from the ocean floor. Its flexible arms and strong claws could handle anything from a delicate shell, to a large boat anchor. Maneuvering it underwater was like flying a plane. And, although Tyler was the best, Alena wasn't a bad pilot in a pinch. She pushed pedals, and turned handles. The Claw circled around to the rear of the sub.

"Mira las garras!"

"Look at those claws! It is coming after us!"

"¡Peligro! Estamos en gran peligro!"

The Claw's long, mechanical arms stretched out. Its powerful claws gripped the drive shaft near the propeller of the sub, and gave a twist. Even from the safety of the *Sea Worthy* Alena and Addison could hear the wrenching, grinding sound of metal being torn apart.

They watched through The Claw's high-definition camera as the enemy submarine began spinning wildly out of control. The propeller shaft vibrated so violently it twisted completely off. The sub became still and then slowly rose to the surface of the bay. They rushed on deck, and Alena turned on a powerful spotlight. The wind and rain slowly pushed the helpless vessel toward the rocky beach.

Finally, able to relax for a minute, Addison turned to Alena. "So. Where's Tyler?"

FIFTEEN

OVERBOARD

A hatch at the top of the steps opened out onto the long bow. The wind had picked up. The deck was slick from the rain, which was coming down even heavier now. The tropical rain was turning into a tropical storm. Lights showed a litter of diving equipment scattered over the deck: scuba tanks, compressors, discarded wetsuits, masks, fins, lengths of chain, weights, and rope. Tyler and Show had to slow down to keep from tripping. Behind them, the hatch banged open, and the men came leaping through. At the same time, two more crew members came running down the side walkway. All of them stopped when they saw Tyler and Show, then they started walking slowing toward them.

"Ven aqui. Ven aquí niña," one of them called, motioning come here with his hand. He was smiling. A smile Tyler didn't like at all.

The edge of the deck was protected on both sides with safety lines that came together at the point of the bow. There was nowhere for them to go. They were trapped, being herded, just like the baitfish are herded by the big predators.

The sailors rushed toward them.

Tyler grabbed two pairs of fins and a scuba tank with its regulator still attached. He grinned at Show, who couldn't help but grin back. "Just like in the movies," he yelled over the noise of the storm.

She plucked up two masks. "Just like," she yelled back.

Holding hands, they vaulted off the ship into the middle of the stormy sea.

* * * * *

There is so much gold. It is so heavy, my back is aching. It is hard carrying it through this thick jungle. The others are aching and complaining, too. But we dare not stop until Captain Benito says. He is not called "Bloody Sword" for nothing. Also, he is clever. Who but the Captain could have tricked away the gold so easily? The guards from Ciudad, Mexico were taking it down to Acapulco. We easily overpowered them, donned their uniforms, and loaded the gold onto the Relampago. No one stopped us. No one asked questions. Así de fácil! And no one was killed. Very unusual for Bloody Sword. But now there is nowhere to spend our treasure. Too many soldiers look for us. That is why we have sailed such a distance to this island of the coconuts, this Isla del Cocos. And why we hide our treasure. We will come back later, when it is safe.

At last we reach the special rock and the twisted tree. And the deep hole above the high tide mark. This will be the last trip. All the gold is here now. The men in front lower their heavy loads into the hole. For a moment, the blanket in which I carry the treasure gapes open. The glitter is bright in the midday sun. So bright it takes my breath away!

As we shovel the dirt, I dream of how I will spend so much. I dream of la hermosa casa I will have on the hilltop. The biggest house in all of Acapulco! Que será maravilloso!

Finally, we are finished. The gold and jewels are buried.

Since I am best with the skill of drawing, I am the one who makes the map. A special honor, the Captain tells me.

He sends the others back to the ship. I sit next to the rock. I begin to draw carefully. The mouth of the bay, the Relampago at anchor, the narrow beach, the tall waterfall, the twisting path worn through the undergrowth, to this rock and this tree. I am careful to draw the rock and the tree well. The gold will be easy to find again. At last I am finished. It is

a good map. I am skilled. I smile at the Captain.

He smiles and takes the map from me. Then he draws his sword...

Tyler woke up to find the storm had passed. Dawn was breaking. *What a weird dream. Where did that come from? Oh, I remember...*

He had been in lots of tight spots before, but last night's ordeal was the most difficult and dangerous he could remember. Waves swamped them, pushing them underwater, tumbling them about. Several times they became separated. They yelled to each other over the storm, and fought their way back together, sharing the air in the scuba tank and thankful for the fins they were wearing. The island, never more than half a kilometer away, slowly, slowly got closer.

Finally, they dragged themselves out of the bay and onto the narrow beach. They found safe shelter under a shelf of rock at the edge of a steep cliff. They huddled together, shivering, and Show talked a little about her time in captivity.

"The crew called him Don Alejandro. They all seemed a little afraid of him." In the darkness, she moved closer. Tyler didn't know if it was from the cold or the remembered fright. "I never knew what they were going to do with me. I tried to make friends with the woman guarding me. She told me his name is Alejandro Benítez. Claims he's the great-great grandson of Benito "Bloody Sword" Bonito, whose real name was Benítez. He is obsessed with the treasure. Calls it his birthright. Says no one can keep it from him."

"That gives him the right to kidnap you and kill hammerheads and mantas?"

As they talked, the worst of the storm passed and they both finally fell into exhausted sleep.

* * * * *

Later, Show was yawning awake. She suddenly sat up. "Where'd it go?"

El Dorado Sueño had disappeared. The bay was empty. "I don't know," Tyler said. "I didn't hear them take off. I just hope Alena made it back in time to alert the Foundation. They could track them. No one should be free to do what they did to you and to this island."

"Speaking of making it back," she said, "let's take a look around, and see just where we are. You know, this island's not completely deserted. It's one of Costa Rica's national parks. Their headquarters is over on Chatham Bay." She seemed to be feeling much better.

It was turning into a beautiful morning. Despite being castaways (temporarily, Tyler hoped), hungry, sore, and tired, he felt great. He'd managed to rescue his friend, and, at least for now, put an end to the senseless underwater explosions that had killed so many beautiful fish.

They climbed awkwardly over jagged rocks scattered at the base of the cliff.

"This landslide is new," Show said. "You can tell by how sharp the edges of the rocks are. And see? Up there? The colors on that part of the cliff are fresh, just like these down here."

"I'll bet the explosions did this," Tyler said. There was a dark shadow behind the jagged rocks. To get by, they had to make their way toward it. Small waves from the bay washed through the rocks under their feet. The shadow was a cave, one of the hundreds that ringed the cliffs around Cocos. This one looked to be newly exposed by the collapse of rocks above. "Be careful. Anything could set off another landslide."

Their path led them into the mouth of the cave. Thin shafts of sunlight highlighted the interior, exposing older rocks, cracks, the ragged roots of long dead plants, and something else – something buried and lost nearly two hundred of years ago.

"Oh, no," Show said.

"Oh, boy," Tyler said.

A stream of bright coins spilled like liquid gold from the cracked and rotted lid of a chest, lying on its side, still half-buried in dirt and rocks.

Feeling like he was still in his dream, Tyler crawled over to the chest

and picked up a coin. It was heavy. Crudely made, jagged around the edges, and minted with dim symbols, still bright and shining after such a long period of time. A jeweled necklace lay half exposed in the chest, with what looked like rubies and diamonds glinting in the shaft of light. Tyler felt his heart beating heavily.

How hard could it be to pull it out? He wedged his hands under the chest and tugged. He was starting to sweat. Am I getting sick? Is this what gold fever feels like? A scattering of pebbles and dirt glanced off his shoulders. He looked up. The top of the cave was lined with cracks.

Then Show called, "It's the *Sea Worthy*! Alena found us! Come on!" The hydroplane was zooming into Wafer Bay. Show ran out and waved her arms to signal Alena where they were, and the boat turned toward her and slowed.

In the cave, Tyler pulled on the chest again.

They both heard the crack overhead.

"Tyler! Get out of there!"

A rock fell and struck him on the leg. He let go of the chest, backing away quickly. We can always come back, he thought.

The dingy grounded on the beach. Show and Tyler tumbled aboard. Tyler quickly introduced Show and Addison. Addison grinned at Show and said, "Nice to meet you, finally." Then they pushed off and bounced through the small waves back to the *Sea Worthy*.

Behind them, they heard a loud rumble and a long cracking sound. They all turned around to watch as the face of the cliff came apart, covering the cave, and spilling into the water in a rush of dirt, boulders, and trees.

SIXTEEN

THE TREASURE OF COCOS ISLAND

The water was blue, the sun was bright. The food was good. The news was better.

"Alena said El Sueño Dorado was taken under tow by the Costa Rican navy this morning," Tyler said, buckling on his weight belt.

"And Benítez?" Show said, adjusting her air tanks.

"He won't be blowing stuff up and killing fish for a long, long time."

Show let out a sigh of relief.

Tyler looked a little worried. "You sure this is a good idea?"

Show smiled and nodded. She was still recovering emotionally from her captivity, but knew that the best therapy in the world was the boundless freedom she felt while diving.

They rolled off the Poco Gitana's rail into the warm, clear water.

The old, rough coin sat in the middle of the table in the *Sea Worthy*'s lounge, winking in the sunlight, as though with a secret.

Addison picked it up and turned it over in his hand. "This is all he found?"

Alena nodded. "There was more. This is all he got out with."

"And now with that landslide, it's gone forever."

The girl gave a curious smile. "Nothing's forever."

Tyler and Show swam deeper, stopping to gaze at a giant manta slowly swimming past. Its wide, powerful wings moving and flexing so gracefully it was like slow motion flying. In the distance, a school of hammerheads was approaching. So beautiful, and so strange. Their long bodies and wide heads silhouetted by the sun above. All around them, the undersea world of Cocos was alive, colorful, forever moving, forever fascinating. The girl began to put the trouble of the past days behind her, letting the wonder fill her, gladdened by the knowledge that they had helped save the wild beauty of the hammerheads and countless other creatures for others to learn about and love, as she loved them.

And, swimming next to her, the boy realized: This is the real treasure of Cocos Island.

GLOSSARY

Autopilot
A system used to guide a vehicle without assistance from a human being. Used extensively on airplanes, it is also used on ships and spacecraft.

Baitball
This phenomenon occurs when small bait fish, upon being hunted, seek protection by forming a furiously spinning silvery ball. This is an attempt of a small species to intimidate and confuse a predator. Sometimes the bait fish will be trapped between the surface and the hunters below. This is when the birds will join the feast. These special events can happen anywhere and at anytime.

Circumnavigate
To sail or fly around.

Dingy
A type of small boat, often carried by a larger boat. Used to go from a ship at anchor to the shore, or from one ship to another.

Galley
On a boat, the kitchen.

GPS
The Global Positioning System is a navigation system using a series of orbiting satellites to track and broadcast microwave signals to determine an object's precise speed, location, and time. Civilian GPS devices can determine positions to within about 15 meters anywhere on the planet.

Head
On a boat, the bathroom.

Helm's a-lee
A sailing term used to mean tacking or coming about, the maneuver by which a sailing boat turns its bow (the forward part of the boat) through the wind so that the wind changes from one side to the other.

Holographic
Holography is a way of showing an image so that the image changes as a viewer looks at it from different positions. A 3-D hologram would allow the viewer to move around the image (or to turn the image) so that it can be viewed from every side.

HUD
Stands for heads-up display, An advanced, transparent display technology that presents information without obstructing the user's view.

Hydrophone
A microphone designed to be used underwater for recording or listening to underwater sounds.

NOAA
The National Oceanic and Atmospheric Administration. A United States government agency that monitors the condition of the oceans and the atmosphere. Its work extends from the surface of the sun to the depths of the ocean floor. NOAA issues regular weather reports, storm warnings, and information on earthquakes.

Rebreather system
For underwater diving, a type of breathing system that uses oxygen and recycled exhaled air. A rebreather is lighter, and more compact than a standard SCUBA system. It gives off almost no bubbles, and is very quiet.

Scalloped hammerhead
A large hammerhead shark with a moderately high first dorsal fin and low second dorsal and pelvic fins. The scalloped hammerhead is uniformly gray, gray-brown, or olive on the dorsal surface, fading to white on the ventral surface and its pectoral fins are tipped with gray or black ventrally.

Sonar
Stands for Sound Navigation and Ranging. Sonar uses sound waves underwater to navigate, communicate, and detect other vessels

Simon Bolivar (1783 - 1830)
An important leader in Spanish America's successful fight for independence from Spain.

Tiller
A lever used to turn a rudder and steer a boat.